You Are Special, Daniel Tiger!

adapted by Angela C. Santomero
based on the screenplays "You Are Special" written by Becky Friedman
and "Daniel Is Special" written by Angela C. Santomero
poses and layouts by Jason Fruchter

Simon Spotlight
New York London Toronto Sydney New Delhi

It's a beautiful day in the neighborhood, and Daniel Tiger is getting ready for school. Daniel is excited because Teacher Harriet has a special surprise planned for today. "Hi, neighbor," says Daniel. "Want to come for a trolley ride to school with me?"

Daniel loves Trolley. Daniel and Mom sing as they ride around the neighborhood to school, *"We're off to school today to play, learn, and sing. Won't you ride along with me? Ride along!"*

Daniel waves to his neighbors as he rides by. "Hi, Music Man Stan! Hi, Dr. Anna! Hi, Baker Aker! Hi, Mr. McFeely!"

"Hi, Daniel! Have a great day at school!" say the neighbors.

"Hello, Daniel Tiger!" says Teacher Harriet. "Come into the classroom and get ready for our special surprise!"

Daniel walks into school, puts his backpack in his cubby, and skips over to his friends. "This is going to be grr-ific," says Daniel.

Daniel and his friends don't have to wait very long to find out about the surprise. "Today we are going to put on a show!" explains Teacher Harriet. "Think of something special that you can do, and then stand on the stage and show it to your friends."

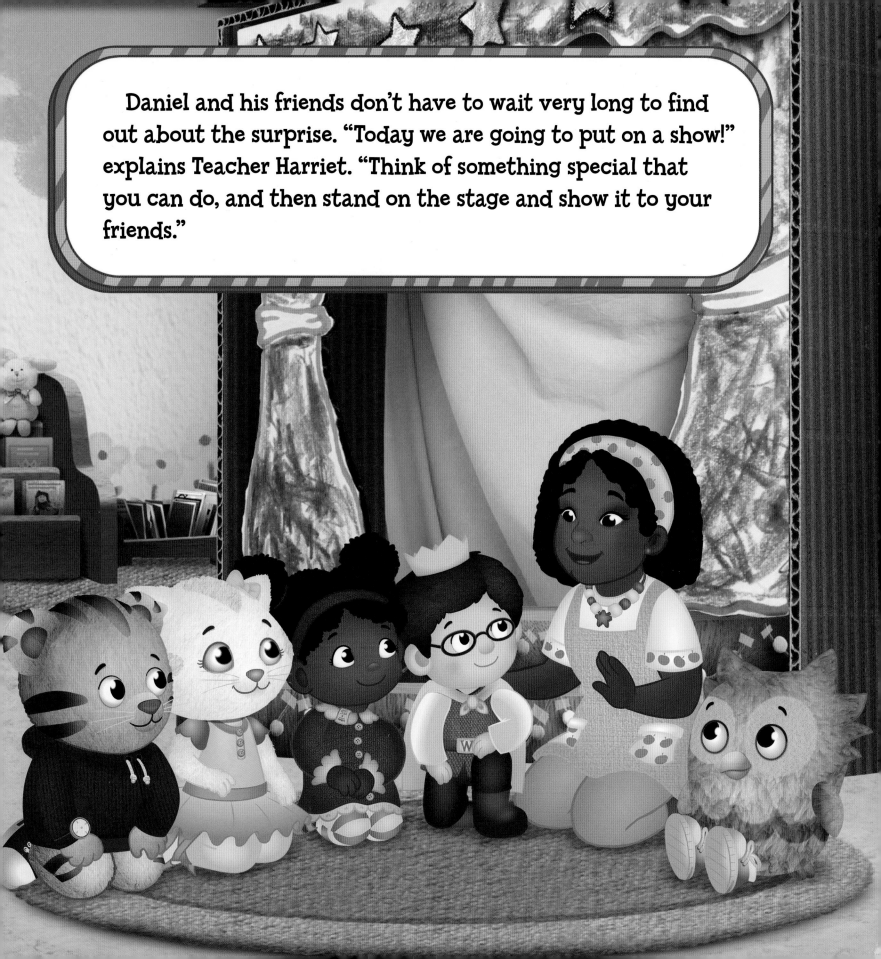

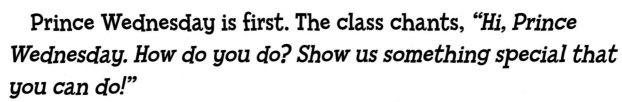

Prince Wednesday is first. The class chants, *"Hi, Prince Wednesday. How do you do? Show us something special that you can do!"*

Prince Wednesday exclaims, "I'm going to do a magic trick! Ready? Ta-da!" Prince Wednesday makes a rubber duck appear out of a hat.

Everyone cheers! Hurray for Prince Wednesday!

Katerina is up next. The class chants, *"Hi, Katerina. How do you do? Show us something special that you can do!"*

Katerina says, "Meow meow, I'm going to twirl on the stage!" Katerina twirls and leaps like a ballerina. She says, "Twirling is my special thing, meow meow!"

Everyone cheers! Hurray for Katerina!

O the Owl is sad. "I don't think I can do anything special, hoo hoo. I don't know any magic like Prince Wednesday and I can't twirl like Katerina," O tells Daniel.

Daniel tells his friend, "You are special, O the Owl."
Then he sings, *"I like you, I like you, I like you just the way you are."*

It's Miss Elaina's turn. The class chants, *"Hi, Miss Elaina. How do you do? Show us something special that you can do!"*

Miss Elaina says, "This is my sheep puppet. Acting with puppets is my super-special talent." Miss Elaina acts out a silly play. The class loves her puppet show—it's so funny!

Everyone cheers! Hurray for Miss Elaina!

It's Daniel's turn next. Just before he steps on stage, Daniel imagines himself putting on a big singing show with Tigey and all of his friends, singing and dancing as the audience cheers him on.

Daniel goes on stage and feels a little bit nervous. His friends chant, *"Hi, Daniel Tiger. How do you do? Show us something special that you can do!"*

Daniel says, "Singing makes me feel special. Here's my song: *My name is Daniel. Daniel Tiger. And I like to sing. La La La. My name is Daniel. Daniel Tiger. And I like my friends, just the way they are."*

Daniel says, "O the Owl, you're smart and fun and you can read books and play the drums and do science experiments! You are special, O. And you are our friend."

Now O is smiling! "Thank you for helping me feel better," he says. "I think I know just what to do for my special talent."

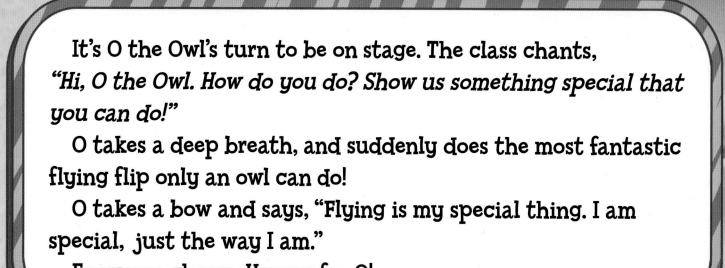

It's O the Owl's turn to be on stage. The class chants, *"Hi, O the Owl. How do you do? Show us something special that you can do!"*

O takes a deep breath, and suddenly does the most fantastic flying flip only an owl can do!

O takes a bow and says, "Flying is my special thing. I am special, just the way I am."

Everyone cheers. Hurray for O!

After the show, Dad comes to pick up Daniel from school. Daniel loves spending time just with Dad. Dad sings, *"You are special to me. You are the only one like you, my friend. I like you. There's only one YOU in this wonderful world. You are special."*

Daniel feels very special. He says, "I love you, Dad."

"I love you, too," Dad says.